First U.S. Edition 1991

First published in Great Britain in 1990
by Hodder and Stoughton Children's Books

ISBN 0-316-41884-6

Library of Congress Catalog Card Number 90-50387

10 9 8 7 6 5 4 3 2 1

Printed in Italy

THREADBEAR

MICK INKPEN

Little, Brown and Company
Boston   Toronto   London

Ben's bear was called Threadbear. He was old. Bits of him had worn out. Or worked loose. Or dropped off.

He had a paw that didn't match and a button for an eye. When he looked through the button he saw four pictures instead of one. It was like looking in a television store window.

But there was one thing that had always been wrong with Threadbear. The silly man who had made him had put too much stuffing inside him. His arms were too hard. His legs were too hard. And there was so much stuffing inside his tummy that his squeaker had been squashed. It had never squeaked. Not even once.

Threadbear hated having a squeaker in his tummy that wouldn't squeak. It made him feel that he was letting Ben down.

Ben's frog could croak. His space monster could squelch. And his electronic robot could burble away for hours if its batteries were put in right.

Even the little toy that Ben called Gray Thing could make a noise, and nobody knew what Gray Thing was supposed to be!

Nobody could make Threadbear's squeaker work.

Ben's dad couldn't do it.   His mom couldn't do it.

Nor could his aunt or his grandma.

Nor could any
of his friends.

When Ben had measles he even asked the doctor about Threadbear's squeaker.

The doctor listened to Threadbear's tummy. But there was no squeak. Not the faintest sign of one.

The other toys tried to help.

"If you had a winder like me, we could wind you up," said Frog.

"If you were made of rubber like me, we could squelch you," said the space monster.

"If you had batteries like me, we could turn you on," said the robot. It was not much help.

"Why don't you ask Santa Claus?" said Gray Thing. "He knows all about toys."

This was a brilliant idea and Gray Thing turned a little pink with pride.

"But where does Santa Claus live?" asked Threadbear.

"At a place called the North Pole," said Gray Thing. "You can get to it up the chimney, I think."

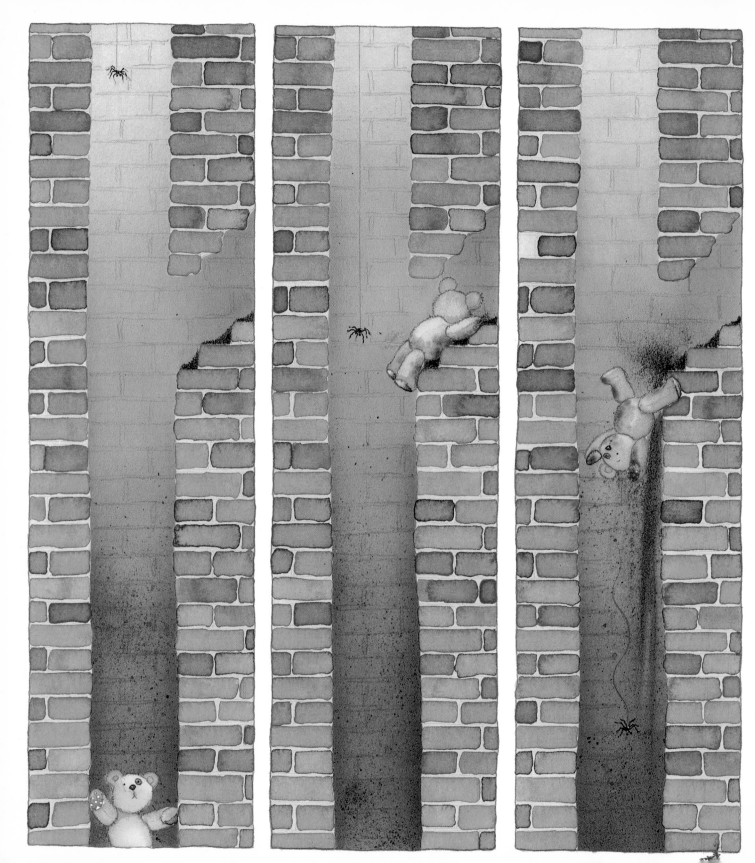

Threadbear had never climbed up a chimney before. It was hard work. He took a wrong turn and fell back down. But he did not give up.

It was long after bedtime when Threadbear poked his head out of the chimney.

This must be the North Pole!

Threadbear sat down to wait for Santa Claus. He waited and waited. But Santa did not seem to be coming.

The moon rose into the sky and Threadbear began to doze....

Threadbear felt himself
falling and falling…

Suddenly Santa Claus was there
helping Threadbear into his sleigh!

It tasted delicious but it made
Threadbear feel sleepy.

They flew over the top of the world and on to the land where the squeaker trees grow.

Threadbear could hear the squeaker
trees as they came in to land.

"You must eat the biggest squeaker fruit,"
said Santa.

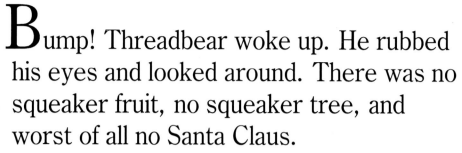

Bump! Threadbear woke up. He rubbed his eyes and looked around. There was no squeaker fruit, no squeaker tree, and worst of all no Santa Claus.

"I must have fallen asleep and dropped off the North Pole!" said Threadbear.

In the morning Ben was surprised to find Threadbear in the garden covered with soot. Ben's mom put Threadbear right into the washing machine. She did not even look at the label on Threadbear's neck, which read in capital letters DO NOT WASH!

When Threadbear came out of the washing machine the soot was gone, but there was a curious purple stain on his chin, which nobody could explain. Threadbear was feeling too dizzy to notice. His head felt like a spinning top!

"I don't mind feeling dizzy," thought
Threadbear as he hung on the line.
"I don't mind having a button for an
eye and a paw that doesn't match.
I don't even mind being hung up by the
ear. But what I DO mind, what I mind
VERY MUCH, is having a silly
squeaker in my tummy
that won't SQUEAK!"

Threadbear was so loud that he
frightened a robin. It flew away, leaving
him alone in the garden bouncing angry
little bounces on the clothesline.

The sun rose slowly over the garden.
It shone straight down on Threadbear,
a great warm shine like an enormous hug.
Threadbear began to steam. He began to
feel better. The more he steamed the
better he felt.

He swung his legs backward and
forward. Then he kicked them high in the
air. Soon he was swinging around and around
the clothesline giggling to himself.

"Why do I feel so happy?" he wondered.

It was at this moment that Threadbear realized a very odd thing had happened to him. His paws felt different. So did his arms and his legs. They were no longer hard!

And inside his tummy was a wonderful, loose, comfortable feeling that he had never felt before!

At the very same moment something caught Threadbear's eye. Something red was racing across the sun. And to Threadbear's surprise the red something was waving goodbye!

When Ben came out to see
if Threadbear was dry he
noticed that his little brown
bear had changed.
"Look, Mom," said Ben.
"He's turned floppy!"
Ben's mom unpinned
Threadbear's ear. "Oh, dear!" she said.
"His stuffing must have shrunk in the wash!"
Ben looked at Threadbear. "I like him
like that. It makes him look…" but Ben
could not think of the right word, so instead
he gave Threadbear a squeeze.
And for the first time the squeaker
in Threadbear's tummy gave the
loudest,
clearest,
squeakiest…